MW00711189

RUN THAT SUCKER
AT SIX!!!

Also by N. Leigh Dunlap
Morgan Calabresé: The Movie

RUN THAT SUCKER AT SIX!!!

the 2ND MORGAN CALABRESÉ collection

St. Martin's Press
New York

Design by Sharleen Smith

Library of Congress Cataloging-in-Publication Data
Dunlap, N. Leigh.
     [Morgan Calabresé. Selections]
     Run that sucker at six! : the second Morgan Calabresé collection /
  N. Leigh Dunlap.
          p.   cm.
     Selections from the comic strip.
     ISBN 0-312-02951-9
     I. Title. II. Title: Morgan Calabresé.
  PN6728.M66D86 1989
  741.5'973—dc19   89-30095
                                                          CIP

First Edition
10 9 8 7 6 5 4 3 2 1

Dedicated with all my love to:
Susan (Mouse)—Lord what you put up with!

And to:
Caliban—(@#!!*! pesty cat.)

And very special thanks to Robert Dirmeyer (in lieu of my first born, would you settle for my naming my next cat after you?)
And to the supportive and otherwise very nice folks at the Washington Blade and Lambda Rising.

Name: **Morgan Calabresé**

Primary Occupation: **Observation of Contemporary America**

Most Admired Person: **Athol Fugard**

Deepest Wish: **A life-partner**

Favorite Book: **"Where The Wild Things Are"**

Favorite Song: **"The Last Time I Saw Richard"—Joni Mitchell**

Age: **a number is arbitrary & doesn't reflect experience**
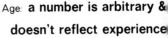

Name: **Phillip Streichler**

Primary Occupation: **Perpetual student of Philosophy**

Most Admired Person: **Jesus—the most misinterpreted man ever**

Deepest Wish: **A cure for AIDS**

Favorite Book: **"The Tibetan Book of the Dead"**

Favorite Song: **Anything by Mitchell. "The Last Time I Saw Richard"**

Age: **31**

Name: **(Rachel) Kyle Keppler**

Primary Occupation: **Performance Artist/Waitress**

Most Admired Person: **Karen Thompson (Martin Luther King, Jr.)**

Deepest Wish: **For compassion to replace "gain" (fame w/dignity)**

Favorite Book: **The National Enquirer ("Audition")**

Favorite Song: **"The Last Time I Saw Richard" ("Blue")**

Age: **29 (can play 16)**

RUN THAT SUCKER AT SIX!!!

HE INSISTS THAT SHE — MUTE, WHEELCHAIR BOUND, ALONE, AND WITHOUT HOPE — MEANT SHE WAS "**HAPPY**" WHEN SHE TYPED-OUT THAT SHE IS "GAY."

DONALD KOWALSKI: THE MAN WHO BELIEVES IT'S BETTER TO BE A VEGETABLE THAN A FRUIT. JOIN US.

HALLOWEEN. FOR CENTURIES, IT HAS BEEN A UNIQUELY GAY HOLIDAY. CHANNEL EIGHT ASKS...WHY?

I'D SAY IT'S A REFLECTION OF OUR CREATIVE NATURE. IT'S A CELEBRATION OF OUR HISTORIC SUPREMACY IN THE ARTS.

WELL, AH, MAYBE BECAUSE OUR VERY SURVIVAL HAS SOMETIMES DEPENDED ON OUR BEING MASTERS OF DISGUISE.

BECAUSE LIKE THE PAGANS
WHO FIRST CELEBRATED
THIS HOLIDAY, WE'RE ONLY
SAFE FROM THE CHRISTIANS'
FLAMES BY DANCING IN
DARKNESS, LOVING IN SECRET.

I WOULD SAY IT'S BECAUSE
EVEN THE MOST POLITICALLY
CORRECT AMONG US MUST
OCCAISIONALLY GIVE-IN
TO A DEEP-SEATED URGE
TO WALLOW IN BAD-TASTE.

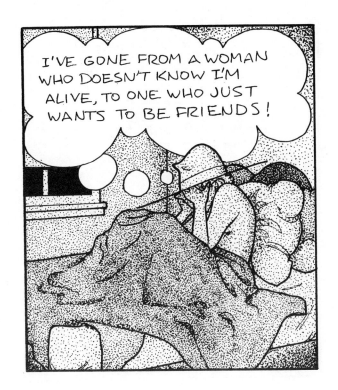

THANKSGIVING WITH FLO WAS, WE DROPPED ACID IN A DORM ROOM SHARED BY A HUMORLESS LIBBER AND AN ACID-QUEEN NAMED FOR A CARTOON CHARACTER.

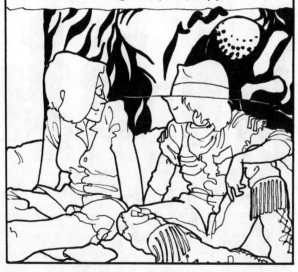

THE ROOM WAS LIKE, THE LEFT AND RIGHT HEMISPHERES OF A BRAIN. IT WAS OKAY IF YOU DIDN'T LOOK AT WHERE THE HALVES MET.

IN THE REC ROOM, WE COOKED CORNISH HENS AND MINIATURE SWEET POTATOES AND SHIT TO LOOK LIKE TEENY-TINY TURKEY DINNERS WE WERE NO WAY REALLY GOING TO EAT.

MY FOLKS CALLED. I THOUGHT IT WAS A GAS THAT THEY WERE, LIKE, "REALLY SORRY THEY COULDN'T HAVE ME HOME, AND THE WHOLE TIME, I'M TRIPPING MY BRAINS OUT WITH A WOMAN I WAS SURE I LOVED.

IN A MOMENT OF REMORSE, MY PARENTS "RE"-OWNED ME FOR THE HOLIDAYS AND WERE STUCK WITH DALE ALMOST THROUGH VALENTINE'S DAY.

WE WERE SHOWN TO A ROOM WITH BUNK BEDS BECAUSE MY FOLKS ASSUMED DALE WAS MY "WOMAN LOVER". THEY WERE CORRECT, BUT THE **ASSUMPTION** BUGGED ME.

WOULD THEY ASSUME EVERY FEMALE GUEST WAS A LOVER? EVERY MORNING, WE MADE THE TOP BUNK LOOK SLEPT-IN TO KEEP THEM GUESSING AND TEACH THEM A LESSON.

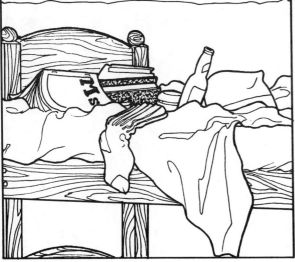

I TREATED THE RELATIONSHIP AS A PARENTAL LEARNING EXPERIENCE. IT TOOK ME THREE YEARS TO LEARN FROM THEM THAT DALE'S **GENDER** WAS NOT THEIR PROBLEM WITH HER.

CHRIS AND I WERE COSMICALLY FATED TO LOVE ETERNALLY. WE MET IN SEPTEMBER, SHARED MEMORIES OF PAST LIVES THROUGH OCTOBER, GREW APART IN NOVEMBER, AND WERE ALMOST FINISHED BY THE HOLIDAYS.

THESE, WE SPENT WITH MY FAMILY. THEY LOVED CHRIS — THEY EVEN TOLD HER SO — BUT I'D COME TO REGARD "SURE THEY LIKE YOU, HON" AS A NECESSARY LIE TO ENABLE YOUR LOVER TO RETAIN HER DIGNITY.

I COULDN'T QUITE ACCEPT THAT IT COULD BE THE TRUTH. I SUPPOSE IT WAS— MY PARENTS' GIFT TO CHRIS WAS THE COMPLETE WORKS OF AYN RAND.

SINCE, AS IT TURNS OUT, OUR LOVE WAS NOT ETERNAL, I'VE NO WAY OF KNOWING IF SHE KEPT THEM. I **DO** KNOW, IF THEY'D COME FROM MY LOVER'S PARENTS TO **ME**, I WOULD— I KNOW THE VALUE OF THAT THOUGHT.

The Kids - Christmas '87

STEVIE AND I SPENT CHRISTMAS CELEBRATING THE WINTER SOLSTICE. IT WAS A COMPROMISE. SHE WOULDN'T HAVE A TREE, BUT I WON STOCKINGS BY CONVINCING HER THEY WERE JUST LITTLE BAGS OF TCHOTCHKES.

WE DIDN'T HEAR FROM MY PARENTS. AROUND PASSOVER, I'D TOLD THEM I MIGHT CONVERT — I WAS KIDDING, CONVERSION IS A LITTLE REDUNDANT WHEN YOU DON'T BELIEVE IN GOD — BUT THAT COULD EXPLAIN IT.

ACTUALLY, I THINK THAT AFTER CHRIS, THEY **BELIEVED** IT WHEN THEY HEARD GAY RELATIONSHIPS NEVER MANAGE TO LAST. SO TO BE CERTAIN THAT THEY WOULDN'T END·UP WASTING PERFECTLY GOOD

EMOTIONAL INVOLVEMENT ON SOMEONE WHO WOULDN'T BE AROUND FOREVER, THEY GAVE OUR RELATIONSHIP A FULL YEAR BEFORE THEY FINALLY WOULD ASK ON THE PHONE," HOW'S... STEVIE, IS IT?" THEY NEVER MET.

CONSTITUTE THE MINIMUM WAGE WORKFORCE; **WE** WHO EXPERIENCE HUMILIATION TO DAILY EXCESS; **WE** WHO SMILE AND SERVE YOU YOUR CAPPUCCINO WHILE YOU TOY WITH THE LATEST IN FEMINIST DOGMA; AND **WE** WHO GET STIFFED BY WOMEN WHO BLOODY WELL OUGHT TO **KNOW** BETTER!!

...I'LL HAVE THE SAME. OH — AND I **HATE** IT WHEN THE CAPPUCCINO SLOSHES OVER THE SIDE INTO THE SAUCER SO DON'T OVERFLOW IT... ME.

ONE A' THESE DAYS, I'M REALLY GONNA' DO IT...

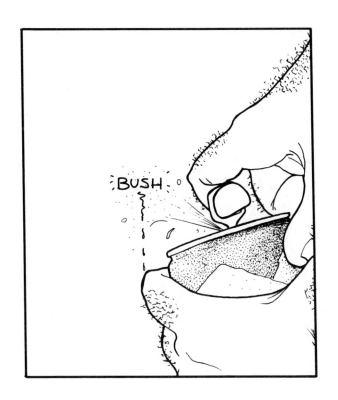

A JUSTICE DEPARTMENT STUDY CONCLUDED THAT LESBIANS AND GAYS ARE THIS NATION'S PRIMARY "HATE CRIME" VICTIMS.

IT WENT ON TO RECOMEND LEGISLATION TO PROTECT A NUMBER OF MINORITIES — INCLUDING LESBIANS & GAYS.

THE U.S. COMMISSION ON CIVIL RIGHTS PASSED THE RESOLUTION — MINUS THE PROVISIONS FOR LESBIANS AND GAYS.

THE COMMISSION EXPLAINED: SUCH LEGISLATION WOULD BE UNPOPULAR SINCE SO MANY PEOPLE HATE LESBIANS & GAYS.

AND SO, TO THE GENTLE STRAINS OF "TURNING IT OVER," WE BID FAREWELL TO YET ANOTHER WOMEN'S MUSIC FESTIVAL SEASON. JOIN US NOW IN REMEMBERING SOME OF THE SEASON'S MOST UNFORGETTABLE MOMENTS.

D-37

THERE WAS THE LAMP IN YOUR TENT WHICH PROVED MORE ILLUMINATING TO YOUR NEIGHBORS,

NATURE CALLED AT 3 A.M, AND THE "SPOT-A-POT" WAS ACROSS THE BALLFIELD, OVER THE HILL, AROUND THE LAKE, PAST THE CABINS, JUST THROUGH THE . . .

REMEMBER THAT BUMP IN THE NIGHT? PROBABLY JUST A RESTLESS "ROWDY" TRIPPING ON TENT STAKES ... OR SO YOU FERVENTLY HOPED...

6 AM. AND ALREADY 92°. YOU REFLECTED BRIEFLY ON THE GREENHOUSE EFFECT, BUT IT FELL TO INSIGNIFICANCE WITH THE DISCOVERY THAT YOU FORGOT TO PACK COFFEE.

111

THE OTHER GUY CARRIED SOME CARDS...
CLAIMED HE WUZ... KENNEDY INSPIRED.
THIS GUY, HE CARRIED THE RIGHT CARDS...
WITH ALL THE MEMBERSHIPS EXPIRED,
AN' WHEN HE SPOKE OF THE FUTURE
HE LEFT US DOUBTFUL AN' TIRED.

AS AH' STARED AT THEM LEVERS...
DAMN NEAR PRAYED FOR SOME LIGHT.
AH' STOOD AN' STARED AT THEM LEVERS...
SAW A TERRIBLE LONG NIGHT.
'CUZ TAKE TWO STEPS TO THE LEFT, NOW...
YOU BE STILL ON THE RIGHT.